MILES ★ LEWIS
TRACK STAR

MILES · LEWIS

TRACK STAR

by Kelly Starling Lyons
illustrated by Wayne Spencer

Penguin Workshop

PENGUIN WORKSHOP
An imprint of Penguin Random House LLC, New York

First published in the United States of America by Penguin Workshop,
an imprint of Penguin Random House LLC, New York, 2023

Text copyright © 2023 by Kelly Starling Lyons
Illustrations copyright © 2023 by Penguin Random House LLC

Visit us online at penguinrandomhouse.com.

Library of Congress Cataloging-in-Publication Data is available.

Manufactured in China

ISBN 9780593383582 (paperback)   10 9 8 7 6 5 4 3 2 1 TOPL
ISBN 9780593383599 (library binding)   10 9 8 7 6 5 4 3 2 1 TOPL

Design by Mary Claire Cruz

For Gabriel, big-hearted
and brave—KSL

For Josie. Who is tiny,
and also ten feet tall.
Keep becoming whoever it is
you're becoming. Oh, and when
life gets muddy, remember to
wear your boots—WS

CHAPTER ONE

On Your Mark

When our bus pulled up at Brookside Elementary, I saw teachers waving and grooving between bright signs: "Go the Distance." "Ready, Set, Race." Even with the windows closed, I could hear party music blaring from speakers. They were pumping us up for the Brookside Fun Run that was happening in two weeks.

Every year, we run laps around the carpool loop. Ten equals a mile. Kyla, Gabi, and RJ ran the most laps in our class last time. My score was somewhere in the middle. This time, I wanted to make the top five.

Fast as a cheetah. Swift as a sailfish. Quick as lightning. That's what I tell myself when I'm in a race. Arms pumping, legs flying, I see myself crossing the finish line like a track star. Usually that gets me going, and I'm proud of how I do.

But when I have to run for a long time, it's like my legs do the opposite. First, they're zooming, and then they're slow as a car about to run out of gas.

"Yes!" my best friend RJ said as he jammed to the music. "I'm definitely getting the most laps this year."

Kyla, who was sitting in front of us, turned and smirked.

"We'll see about that," she said.

RJ and I laughed. This was supposed to be all about fun, but for some kids, it was all about bragging rights. People sponsor us, and we raise money for the school. Classes with the most laps win pizza parties. Kids who bring in the most money can earn passes to cool activities like mini golf and movies. Everyone slurps on Popsicles when they finish running.

As we got off the bus, my heart pounded at the excitement. But why did I have butterflies, too? It's not like it's a big track meet, but I wanted to do better than I did last time. Trying to achieve your best is a big deal in my family. I didn't want to let them and myself down.

In Miss Taylor's room, I tucked my

backpack in my cubby and headed to my seat. She passed out flyers for the Fun Run. We slipped them into our take-home folders.

"This year's theme is Laps for Laptops," Miss Taylor said. "The more we raise, the more new laptops we get for the school."

And we sure needed them. I was in the technology club—the computers we had looked like they were from my parents' day.

Some friends chattered and smiled as they talked about the run, but I saw Carson frowning as he looked the flyer over. He can double Dutch almost as good as Simone, but running is not his thing. The last time we had the Fun Run, he got the least laps in.

Miss Taylor hit the chime to signal the morning meeting.

Chirr! Chirr! it sang, and the talking ended like someone pulled the plug on a TV.

"Okay, class, it's time to get

started," she said. We joined her on the orange-and-blue rug.

"The Fun Run is just in time for our science unit on vitamins, minerals, and exercise. We're going to talk about what we're putting into our bodies, how food gives us energy, and how to live healthier lifestyles. Think about it. What could you do better?"

"Eat less junk food," Jada said.

"Walk more," Gabi added.

I get lots of exercise playing basketball, hockey, and riding my bike, but I get tired out too quickly. I raised my hand.

"What about lasting longer when we run or exercise?"

"Great point," Miss Taylor said. "That's called endurance."

As she filled us in on what we'd be covering, a smile spread across my face. What if I came up with my own set of exercises, something that was guaranteed to make me fast as a flash and last as long as a battery? When the Fun Run came, I'd be ready.

I thought about the run all day and on the bus ride home. After I finished my math homework, I looked at the yellow flyer again.

"You coming, Miles?" Nana asked as she tied her sneakers. I'd promised to go with her on a walk around the neighborhood. Time to put my plan into action.

"Coming!"

We stretched before getting
started. I copied Nana's moves, rolling
my head and shoulders, lunging to
each side, reaching as high as I could
and then touching my toes.

"I feel nice and warmed up," she
said. "How about you?"

I nodded.

"Okey doke, let's go the long way this time."

The long way? Uh-oh. I knew the route Nana was talking about. It's all the way around the neighborhood, down to the grocery store and back. I took a breath and breathed out slowly. No turning back now.

When we started walking, I did okay. I kept up with her, no problem. But then Nana picked up the pace. She was speed-walking, her locs swishing as she zipped down the sidewalk. I huffed and struggled to match her stride.

"You're too young to conk out so quickly," she said, slowing down. "You should come walking with me more."

As I panted and tried to catch my breath, I knew she was right. I had a lot of work to do. If I got tired out walking with Nana, what chance did I have at the Fun Run?

CHAPTER TWO

Get Set

For gym class the next day, Mr. Best took us outside to go through warm-up stations. Each one had a sign listing a different exercise: thirty jumping jacks, fifteen squats, ten torso twists, five push-ups, and more.

"After we finish here, we're going to get in some running practice," he said. "Is everybody ready?"

"Yes!" we cheered.

The stations got me hyped. I
hurried through them and shifted
from foot to foot, trying to get
out some of my nervous energy. I
couldn't wait for the practice run to
start.

"Kyla thinks she's going to be

the fastest," RJ said, twisting his lips. "Just watch. She's gonna be my shadow. I did a 5K with my mom last year."

Gabi overheard him.

"I bet Kyla would love to hear that," she said, and walked over to her.

"RJ, your mouth keeps getting you in trouble," I said, shaking my head.

"It's not trouble if you can back it up."

We lined up and walked to the carpool loop. As everyone got ready,

I pictured myself at the start of an important race. I breathed in and out slowly, lowered my head, and got prepared to blast off as soon as I heard Mr. Best's voice.

"Go!"

I'm Usain Bolt. I'm Quicksilver.

That's what I told myself as I pretended my legs were wings. I flew around that loop. The first few laps, I was keeping up with the fastest in my class, but one by one, Kyla, RJ, and Gabi passed me. I pushed myself to speed it up. But it was like my legs had their own plans. I kept slowing down.

I saw other kids struggling, too. Some panted but tried to keep pushing. Some jogged like me. Carson breathed heavily and slowed to a walk.

"I'm worn out, too," I said, walking alongside him. "Want to run together?"

Carson shook his head.

"I'm okay," he said. "I'm gonna walk for a while. You keep going."

I nodded and tried to get back into the groove. The break was just what I needed. I started running again. But when Mr. Best called time, I sighed in relief. My legs ached.

"Great job, everyone," he said as we guzzled water. "Wonder why some of you tired out so quickly?"

We looked at one another as if the answer was on our faces.

"You have to pace yourself," he said. "This isn't a sprint. If you start running at full speed, it's tough to keep that momentum all the way through."

What Mr. Best said made sense. I hadn't thought of that. I wanted to be fast, but maybe the key was starting out slower. Like Nana—she walked at first and then built up to going quicker.

"RJ, didn't you say I was going to be your shadow?" Kyla said.

"Whatever, Kyla," he said and turned his head.

Kyla dusted him this time, but I knew it wasn't over. RJ was as competitive as she was. Neither was going to give up. They would keep trying to be the top.

Back in Miss Taylor's class, she handed out a list of different foods.

"Okay, friends, I want you to check off the ones you eat."

As I scanned the options, I saw some of my favorites like ice cream, burgers,

- burgers
- ice cream
- french fries
- cake
- fresh fruit and vegetables
- yogurt
- beans
- whole grains

french fries, and cake on
the left. I had the same number
of checks on that side as I did on
the right side with fresh fruit and
vegetables, yogurt, beans, and
whole grains.

"We get more energy and
nutrition from the food on the right,"
Miss Taylor said. "It's okay to have
the ones on the left for special treats,
but you shouldn't eat them all the
time."

Simone raised her hand.

"Call me 'Cookie Monster,'" she
said, imitating him gobbling up
treats.

"Okay, Cookie Monster," Miss
Taylor said, laughing. "I didn't say

you had to give them up. But I want you to think more about what goes into your body. What's going to give you energy and make you stronger?"

Eating differently wasn't going to be part of my plan to get more laps in at the Fun Run. But maybe it should be. Exercising and walking more would help, but eating more healthy foods could give me the boost I needed to succeed.

At lunch, I got in the line and asked for the chicken and a double helping of sweet potatoes and broccoli. Usually, I got a cookie for dessert. I skipped it this time.

I sat in my usual spot between RJ and Jada. I munched my food and watched my friends gobble goodies

like ice-cream bars and fruit snacks. I wasn't even jealous. I took another bite of broccoli and focused on my goal. Nothing was going to stop me from doing my best this year.

CHAPTER THREE

Game Plan

When I got home from school, Dad was there instead of Nana. I took off my shoes by the door and noticed her blue sneakers were missing.

"Did Nana already leave for her walk?"

"Yep, you just missed her."

"Aw," I said, groaning. "I'm trying to get ready for the Fun Run. Nana

was helping me train."

"That's what's up," Dad said, holding out his fist for a pound. "Proud of you. Ever heard of Sifan Hassan or Earl Johnson?"

Here it comes. Dad was a Black history professor—he loved sharing facts about heroes I should know. I shook my head.

"When you get a chance, look them up. You just might be inspired."

I nodded and hit the stairs.

"Hey, Miles, I have some time since my last class was canceled," he said. "Want to ride bikes?"

He didn't have to ask twice.

"Sure!"

I slipped on my sneakers and met him in the garage. We put on our helmets. Then, it was time to fly.

Dad took off first. I remembered him and Mom teaching me how to ride my bike. At first, I kept wobbling and putting my feet on the ground. I just couldn't get my balance. I wondered if I'd ever get the hang of it. Then, one day, everything they

told me clicked.

Now look at me, keeping pace right behind Dad. I grinned as the wind whooshed in my face, and we pedaled down our neighborhood streets. I didn't even get nervous when we reached hills anymore.

I used to have to get off and walk my bike up them. Now, I just relaxed, used my leg muscles, and made it the top. If I could master bike riding, maybe I could ace running, too.

As we rode, we saw a familiar person with silver-streaked locs speed-walking.

"Hey, Nana," I called out.

She waved and blew a kiss, but she kept moving. Nana didn't let anything get her off her game.

Back at home, I looked up the people Dad had talked about. Sifan Hassan is an Ethiopian-Dutch long-distance runner. She won two

gold medals and one bronze at the 2020 Olympics in Tokyo. She holds the women's world record for the mile. Earl Johnson was the first Black American distance runner to get a national ranking. They both trained hard, focused on their goals, and made them come true. As I thought about what they achieved, I remembered an inspiring runner who was right in my family.

Weekday mornings, my mom leaves when it's still dark, wearing her athletic gear and sneakers. She meets her running group to get in a mile before work. Together they've done 5Ks, 10Ks, and even a half-marathon, which is about thirteen miles! She would be the best person to ask for tips.

"Mom, how did you get so good at running?" I asked after dinner.

She laughed.

"You should have seen me when I was your age. You would have thought I was allergic to running. I got worn out just thinking about it."

I couldn't believe that. I never knew a time when she didn't do it.

"It was hard at first. I did lots of walking and built up my stamina. Slowly, I started to jog. Then, as I got stronger, I was able to run for longer.

You have to take it bit by bit. You'll get there."

Sounded like Mom becoming a better runner took months. I only had two weeks until the Fun Run. I had to hurry. That meant working harder on my plan.

"Can I go running with you this weekend?" I asked.

"Sure," she said. "I like to get out early before it's hot. You sure you can hang?"

"Definitely," I said, though I wasn't so sure.

Hang with Mom? Hoped I was ready.

CHAPTER FOUR

Practice Makes Progress

Mom wasn't playing when she said "early." On Saturday morning, it was just us and the birds chirping hello on our street. I hopped into Mom's car for our run in the park.

"Okay, Miles," she said. "We'll start off walking to warm up. Then, we'll jog and do some running. I'm proud of you for trying to do more laps and

earn money for your school."

I didn't tell her I had another reason. Getting more laptops was great, but I wanted to prove to myself I could be faster and last longer. Being first didn't matter, but giving it your all was something my family expected. Mom said when she faces a challenge she always tries to "show up and show out." I wanted to do that, too.

When we pulled up at the park, I was surprised that the lot wasn't empty. Looked like lots

of people were out getting exercise. We grabbed our water bottles and started for the trail.

I saw dads chatting while pushing strollers. Teens walked dogs and talked. Two ladies who reminded me of Nana were running while using earbuds. They were all in.

As we strolled along the trail, I saw squirrels dashing up trees and ducks gliding across the lake.

"Okay, Miles," Mom said. "Time to pick up the pace."

We started jogging. It felt good at first, but after a while, I panted and slowed down. Mom noticed me struggling.

"Remember to breathe," she said.

I breathed and drank some water. That helped a lot. But then the thoughts came. *What is wrong with me? Why can't I last as long as Mom? Will I ever get it together?*

Mom looked at me frowning and could tell I needed a boost.

"Did you learn about the tortoise and the hare in school?" she asked.

I nodded.

"Do you remember the moral?"

"Slow and steady wins the race."

"Focus on that," she said. "Start off even and slow."

We jogged for a while longer.

"Ready to run?"

I took a deep breath and nodded. As we ran back to the start of the trail, I remembered what Mom said about hating running when she was younger. Weird to imagine Mom having a hard time keeping up, just like Carson and me. You'd never know it now. But thinking about her having trouble gave me strength. I breathed and pushed myself to keep going. If she could do it, I could, too.

★

At school that week, I was ready
for gym class. I got tips from Mom.
I was eating better. I didn't rush

through the warm-up stations like I did before. I took my time and did them each the best I could.

Whenever Mr. Best called for us to line up to practice for the Fun Run, I remembered that tortoise Mom talked about. *Slow and steady*, I repeated to myself.

"Go!"

My friends blasted off the line like last time, but I found my own flow. I jogged slowly and then put on the speed toward the last few laps.

"Much better," Mr. Best said when he called time. "Saw some good improvement, Miles," he added.

I grinned that he'd called me out for praise.

"Who dusted who this time?" I heard RJ whisper to Kyla.

She rolled her eyes. Those two. They were still determined to race at top speed as much as they could. I don't know if anything would stop them from wanting to get the most laps.

I noticed that Carson had his head down. He had struggled as we ran and ended up walking for a lot of it. I got an idea.

"Hey, Carson," I said. "Want to walk laps at recess? I could use some more practice."

"Sure, I guess I could," he said.

Usually I played kickball, but helping Carson came first. Maybe it would help me more, too. After lunch, we headed back outside. Friends raced to double Dutch, kickball, and basketball. Carson and I started walking around the field.

"My mom has been helping me train," I said. "Remember that fable Miss Taylor read to us about the tortoise and the hare? Mom said we should follow that lesson: Slow and steady wins the race."

We took our time at first just like I did with Mom.

"Ready to jog?"

Carson nodded. We stayed side by side. Every day that week, we did that routine. Mr. Best noticed the improvement.

"Way to go, Carson," Mr. Best said on Friday. He jogged the whole time and even ran the last lap.

At recess, Carson challenged me to a race.

"Let's see who can get to the double Dutch area first," he said.

"You're on!"

As we ran to where Lena and Simone were twirling ropes, Carson grinned and put on the gas. Arms swinging, legs speeding like a train, he was hard to catch.

"Let's call it a tie," I said.

It felt good passing on what I learned. And I still had time to get some kickball in.

"Miles, you want to jump?" Carson asked.

"Me?" I said. "Nah. I don't know how."

"That's okay," he said. "You taught me something. Let us teach you. Watch."

Lena and Simone turned and Carson easily ran into the ropes. His feet danced back and forth. He kept up no matter how fast the ropes flew. Then, he ran out. I was impressed.

"Your turn," he said.

Simone and Lena got the ropes moving. I kept waiting for my chance to jump in.

"Don't be afraid of the ropes," Carson said. "Watch the rhythm and give it a try."

They slowed down the turning.

"Ready, set, go!" Carson gave me
a cue.

I ran into the ropes and started
jumping. I did it! I couldn't believe
I was keeping up. Jada and Carson
cheered. Then, I tried to get fancy.

"Faster," I said.

They gave me what I wanted. One, two. One, two. Left foot. Right foot. This wasn't so bad. One . . . I missed. All I saw was a tangle of ropes and felt my legs hitting the ground.

"You okay?" Carson asked.

I nodded until I stood up.

"Ow," I moaned. My leg ached a little. It wasn't terrible, but it felt sore.

Jada ran to Miss Taylor. She came over to check on me. When she touched my leg and applied some pressure, I winced.

"We better have the school nurse check it out," she said. "Carson, go with Miles."

We were quiet at first as we made our way down the hall.

"I'm sorry, Miles," Carson said. "I didn't mean for that to happen."

I nodded without making eye contact. I wasn't mad at Carson. I was mad at myself, but I didn't feel like talking.

Nurse Williams, the school nurse, looked over my leg and checked my ankle.

"You have a bruise forming on your leg," he said. "You must have hit the ground pretty hard. Let's put some ice on it so it doesn't swell. I'm going to send a note home suggesting that you take a break from exercise for a couple of days."

No exercise? It was almost time for the Fun Run!

He must have seen the panic on my face.

"Don't worry," Nurse Williams said. "You'll be ready for Monday's big event. Just take it a little easy until then."

How could I take it easy? I needed all the practice I could get. I couldn't believe this had happened. Would all my hard work be for nothing?

When I came out of the nurse's office, Carson was waiting.

"Are you going to be okay?" he asked.

"I don't know," I snapped.

I saw his face fall. But I kept going. I had worked hard and was almost at my goal. This stunk.

"I never should have double Dutched. I don't know why I didn't just go to kickball. Now, everything is messed up."

Carson looked down. We walked back to class without saying a word.

CHAPTER FIVE

Mind and Body

Nurse Williams was right. I had a big bruise on my leg. On Saturday, it didn't ache as much. But I still had to rest it. That hurt more than the pain of falling. I had the worst luck.

Mom told me Carson called, but I hadn't called him back yet. It wasn't his fault. But thinking about what happened just made me feel bad.

I moped around the house and flopped on the couch. I turned on the TV. There was nothing on I wanted to see. I shook my head and sighed— figures.

"Why are you looking like your bike has a flat?" Nana said.

I frowned.

"I was doing so good with getting ready for the Fun Run," I said and hit the couch pillow next to me. "Now, I can't do anything. It's not fair."

"That pillow didn't do anything to you," she said.

"Nana," I said, faking a complaint about her joke.

"Am I wrong?" she said, smiling. "I know you're disappointed. But preparation is not just physical. It's what you put in your mind, too. I have mantras that I use when I want to reach a goal. I think of a phrase and say it in my mind over and over."

Mantra? Was that what you called it? I knew what Nana was talking about. Before races, I used to picture myself as a track star like Usain Bolt.

"I am Usain Bolt. I am Usain Bolt,"
I would tell myself. That worked
for sprints, but maybe I needed
something different for the Fun Run
since it was so much longer. I thought
about the tortoise from the fable.

"Slow and steady wins the race."

"What did you say?" Nana asked.

I didn't realize I'd said it out loud.

"Slow and steady wins the race,"
I said with confidence.

"There you go," she said. "Practice
that mantra and rest a couple more
days. You'll be ready. Believe that."

Nana walked toward the kitchen.

"How about helping me with
dinner?" she said. "We're having
barbecued chicken and baked sweet

potatoes. What should we have with it?"

"How about salad?"

"Perfect!"

I helped Nana cut up the cucumbers and tomatoes. We tossed them in the bowl with lettuce and shredded carrots and onions. We

sprinkled cheese on top. Then, we made an Italian dressing to go on it.

"Heard you made the salad," Mom said, after finishing a forkful. "Yummy."

"Thanks, Mom!"

"I got some more pledges for you, Miles," Dad said. "Some of my fishing buddies are sponsoring you for the Fun Run."

"Yes!"

"How are you feeling about it?" Mom asked. "Ready?"

I nodded, and I meant it.

"That's great," she said. "Just do your best and have fun. We'll all be there cheering you on."

That night, I dreamed that I was

in the Fun Run. I wasn't stressed. I wasn't huffing and puffing. I ran at my own pace and ruled the track.

Sunday after church, I asked Nana if we could go walking.

"I think that would be okay," Nana said. "Are we taking a quick walk or the scenic route?"

"The long way."

She smiled.

We stretched and then the walk was on. This time, when Nana sped up, I wasn't trailing her. I matched her stride.

"I see you, Miles," she said. "That's how you do it."

I felt confident. I felt ready. Then, I thought about Carson and felt a queasy feeling in my stomach. I acted like it was his fault. That wasn't right. He probably thought I was mad at him. I called his house. No one answered. My heart dropped.

Why had I treated him that way?

CHAPTER SIX

Go Time

The morning of the Fun Run, Dad made strawberry banana smoothies to go with our scrambled eggs and turkey bacon.

"This will give you lots of energy," he said. "Watch out Fun Run, Miles DuBois Lewis is on the case!"

"Let's have a toast," Mom said, raising her glass. "To doing your best," she said.

Clink. We tapped each other's glasses.

On the bus to school, RJ could hardly sit still.

"Can you believe somebody still thinks she's going to get more laps than me?" he said looking at Kyla, who sat on the seat across the aisle.

"Think?" Kyla said. "Don't you mean *know*?"

"Okay, Kyla," RJ said. "We'll see."

I laughed to myself. When this was all over, they would be buddies again. But I didn't have time to think about their competition. I needed to find Carson.

Music filled the air as we neared the school. This time, I saw DJ

Smooth, a friend's mom, mixing tunes under an archway of balloons in our school colors, silver and blue. Colorful signs lined the sidewalk. Teachers jammed and waved pom-poms. The Brookside Fun Run was about to start.

In Miss Taylor's class, Carson's seat was empty. Maybe he was coming late. I hoped I had time to talk to him before it was our grade's turn to run.

Chirr! Chirr!

It was time for morning meeting. We sat on the carpet and waited for announcements. Still no Carson.

"I'm proud of each of you," Miss Taylor said, gazing at our faces. "You've been working hard, rooting for each other. Your run today is really going to help the school."

I hung my head. I started out trying to help but ended up hurting a friend. We weren't back in our seats long before I heard a voice on the intercom.

"Fourth graders, report to the carpool loop."

"Line up, class," Miss Taylor said, grinning. You could feel the energy as everyone buzzed about the run.

Just then, Carson came in. I tried to make eye contact. He looked away.

"Carson, I'm so glad you made it in time," Miss Taylor said. "Put your book bag in your cubby and hop in line."

I was near the front. Carson was in the back. No way we could talk now. All the way down the hall I kept thinking that I had to make it right.

Jada and Simone held the doors open for our class. I saw people everywhere as we walked outside. Teachers, parents, and neighbors were there to cheer us on. Miss Taylor took us to the starting line. Before I could get over to Carson, Mr. Best announced that it was time to begin. I sighed.

Mom, Dad, and Nana waved at me. I waved back. Then, I started saying my mantra in my mind: *Slow and steady wins the race. Slow and steady wins the race.*

"On your mark."

My body tensed. *I can do this. I can do this. I trained and I'm ready.* I focused straight ahead.

"Get set."

I felt my legs tensing. I breathed in and out until they relaxed. It wasn't about going fast—it was about pacing myself and doing my best. The only person I was competing against was me.

"Go!"

Kids exploded around the loop. Kyla and RJ zoomed like they were going for Olympic gold. Not me. I kept my breathing even and ran in a steady stride.

I didn't huff and puff or pant.

I just ran and breathed, exactly like Mom said. Each lap made me feel more confident. I definitely had this.

Then, I spotted Carson up ahead. He was struggling like he had last year. He was doing so good last week. What happened?

"Are you okay?" I asked, walking alongside him.

"Yeah," he said. "I'm surprised you're talking to me."

I watched my classmates rushing by me. If I kept standing there, I might not meet my goal. What was I going to do? I looked at my family cheering for me. *Show up and show out.* That's what Mom always does. I knew I had something to do.

"I'm sorry, Carson," I said. "I didn't mean to take it out on you. I was just upset. I really wanted to do better this year."

"Don't let me stop you," he said.

I looked at Carson again and thought about my mom when she was little, and me last year.

"Nope," I said. "I'm hanging out with you. We can just walk if you want or run when you're ready."

"Really?" he said.

"Yep."

And what do you know? Carson started jogging. I jogged right next to him.

"Go, Carson!" I heard his dad calling out his name. He heard it, too. He held his head higher and started speeding up.

"Race you to the end?" he said.

"You're on!"

As we ran around the loop, the cheers of the crowd were like a roar. Even our classmates were calling out to Carson. RJ and Kyla stopped focusing on each other and ran with us. Before I knew it, our class was in a big group running together.

We didn't care who got the most laps. We were supporting one another.

"Time!"

We jumped up and down. We did it! Coach Best gave Carson a high five.

Carson's smile gleamed like the sun.

"Who's ready for Popsicles?" Miss Taylor said.

"We are!"

As I tore open the paper and dug in, it tasted different than any I'd had before. I looked at my friends and knew this wasn't mango. It was the flavor of success.

Miles's Five Facts

When my dad had me look up Sifan Hassan and Earl Johnson, I learned facts about other Black runners, too. I put a few of them in my notebook.

Here are some of my favorites. Did you know:

1. John Baxter Taylor Jr. was the first African American to win a gold medal in the Olympics. He earned that title in 1908 as part of the one-mile relay team.

2. Wilma Rudolph won three gold medals and broke three world records for track and field at the 1960 Olympics. She was the first

American woman to win three gold medals at the same Olympics and was called "the fastest woman alive."

3. In the '80s, Flo-Jo won two world records for sprints. Her full name was Florence Griffith Joyner. Her sister-in-law, Jackie Joyner-Kersee, was top in the long jump and the heptathlon. For the heptathlon, she had to compete in seven events including long jump, hurdles, running, and more.

4. Usain Bolt, who represents Jamaica, is known as the greatest sprinter of all time. He's the fastest man in the world. I bet he has the coolest name for a runner ever.

5. One of the fastest kids in the world is Rudolph Ingram Jr., who lives in Florida. His nickname is "Blaze." He ran the 100-meter race in 13.48 seconds when he was only seven years old. That was a record for his age group and only a few seconds behind Usain Bolt's time!

Acknowledgments

When I began writing this book, I started with
a question: What does winning really mean?
Everyone has a different answer. For some, it's
coming in first. For others, it's being there for
others. Or maybe it's a combination of doing your
best and showing empathy.

I hope as you read Miles's latest adventure
that you figure out what winning means to
you. I'm inspired by the amazing ways kids like
you face challenges with grace, bravery, and
determination. My children and all of you have
been some of my greatest teachers.

To me, you win when you dare to try, give
a challenge your all, and lead with your heart.
It's not about competing with other people, but
"showing up and showing out" for yourself and
others and letting the hero inside you shine.

It's such a joy to create a book that

celebrates the wonderful friends you are.

Thank you to my insightful editor Renee, gifted illustrator Wayne, and the outstanding Penguin Workshop team for making this series so special. Thank you to my agent, Caryn, and always to my family and friends for their support. And thanks and love to each of you for being great readers and friends. Keep shining!

Want more Miles?
Find him in the
Jada Jones series!